Kid Architect

goes to

INDIANA

Gary Vance, FAIA
with Lauren Vance and Elizabeth Wells

www.KidArchitectBook.com

Copyright #TXu 2-143-252

©2020 All rights reserved. No portion of this book may be reproduced—mechanically, electronically, or by any other means, including photocopying—without written permission of the author.

This book is self published by the authors.

Authored by Gary Vance, FAIA
with Lauren Vance and Elizabeth Wells
Design by Lauren Vance
Illustrations by Gary Vance

Photography copyright of the respective owners, used with permission

First printing May 2020

10 9 8 7 6 5 4 3 2 1

HELLO THERE!

Let me start by introducing myself: my name is Kid Architect! I love all things architecture, landscape architecture, building design and public art, so I'm on a quest to explore and learn everything I can about important buildings around the country.

This book is my journal of all the research I've collected on cool buildings and landscapes in the state of Indiana. Each bulletin board has my notes, thoughts, facts, drawings, and photos to help you learn all about these important buildings and art installations. When you're finished reading about the buildings, give a few of the S.T.E.A.M. activities near the back of the book a try! Also in the back you'll find a glossary of design and construction words, so if you don't know what something means, look it up!

I hope you enjoy learning about these buildings as much as I did. Take the time to appreciate the beauty in landscapes and architecture that surround us every day.

Peace, Love, and Architecture,

-Kid Architect

IMPORTANT BUILDINGS & PUBLIC ART IN INDIANA

Main Building (Golden Dome) (p. 4-5)
University of Notre Dame–South Bend

West Baden Springs Hotel (p. 6-7)
French Lick

Boone County Courthouse (p. 8-9)
Lebanon

Lerner Theatre (p. 10-11)
Elkhart

SAMARA: John and Catherine Christian House (p. 12-13)
West Lafayette

Emens Auditorium and Music Complex (p. 14-15)
Ball State University–Muncie

The Republic Building (p. 16-17)
Columbus

Simon Skjodt Assembly Hall (p. 18-19)
Indiana University–Bloomington

Arts United Center (p. 20-21)
Ft. Wayne

Children's Museum of Indianapolis (p. 22-23)
Indianapolis

Falls of the Ohio Interpretive Center (p. 24-25)
Clarksville

White Chapel (p. 26-27)
Rose-Hulman Institute–Terre Haute

Lucas Oil Stadium (p. 28-29)
Indianapolis

Evansville Museum of Arts, History & Science (p. 30-31)
Evansville

Wilmeth Active Learning Center (p. 32-33)
Purdue University–West Lafayette

Public Art "Love Sculpture" (p. 34)
Located at Newfields–Indianapolis

Public Art "Engineering Fountain" (p. 35)
Located at Purdue University–West Lafayette

Public Art "Convergence" (p. 36)
Located in Promenade Park–Ft. Wayne

Public Art "Roundabout Art" (p. 37)
Located in traffic roundabouts–Carmel

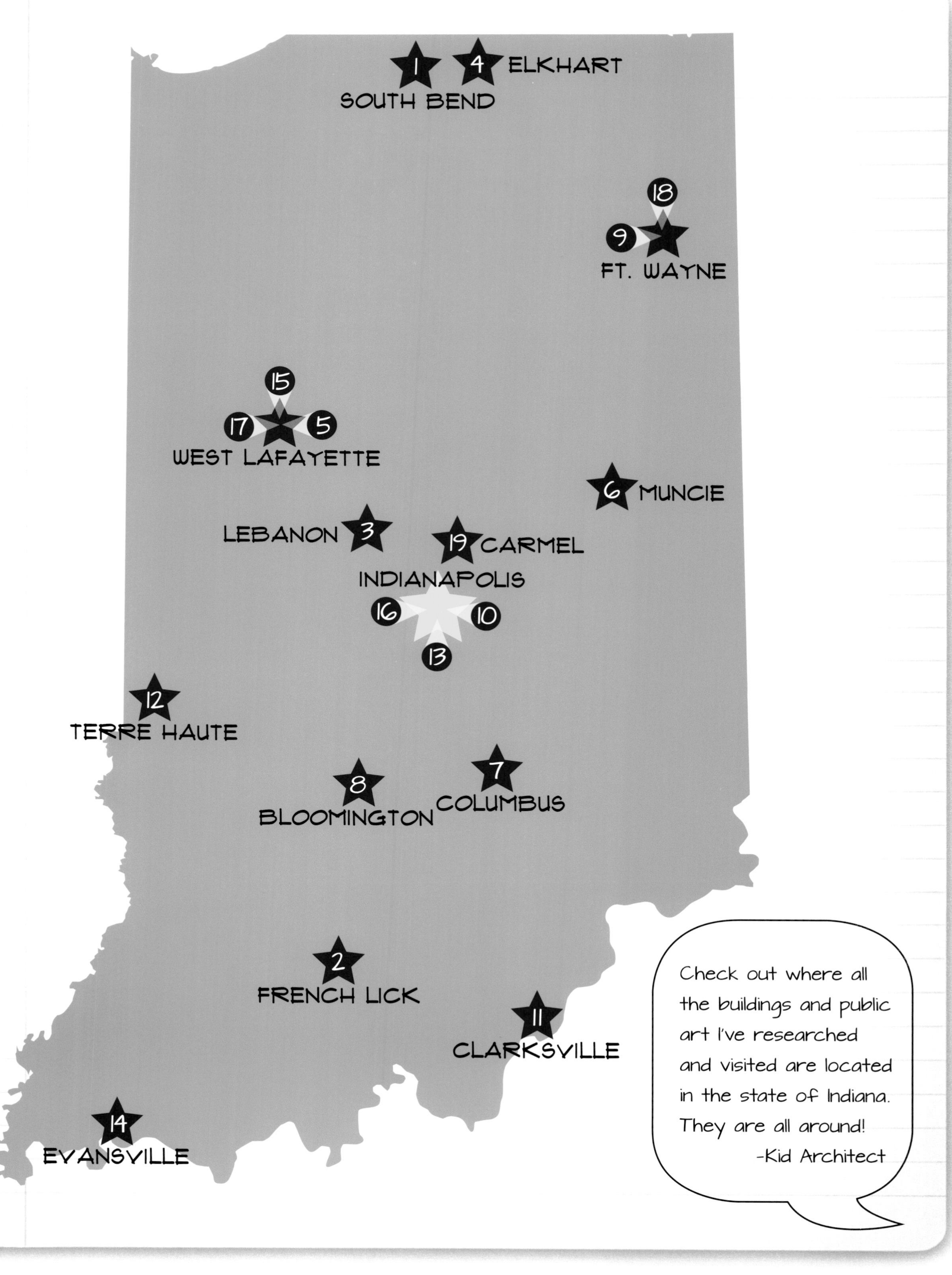
ELKHART
SOUTH BEND
FT. WAYNE
WEST LAFAYETTE
MUNCIE
LEBANON
CARMEL
INDIANAPOLIS
TERRE HAUTE
BLOOMINGTON
COLUMBUS
FRENCH LICK
CLARKSVILLE
EVANSVILLE
Check out where all the buildings and public art I've researched and visited are located in the state of Indiana. They are all around!
-Kid Architect

MAIN BUILDING

ALSO KNOWN AS GOLDEN DOME BUILDING

UNIVERSITY OF NOTRE DAME • SOUTH BEND, INDIANA

Construction on the current building was completed in 1879.

THIS BUILDING IS IMPORTANT BECAUSE...

It is the most recognized building on campus and is the symbol of the University of Notre Dame. The building is at the center (or middle) of the campus, both physically and spiritually, and it is one of the oldest buildings on campus.

It was recognized by and listed on the National Historic Register in May of 1987.

- On top of the dome is a statue of the university namesake: Our Mother, Mary
- Model is a replica of a statue in Rome erected by Pope Pius IX
- The statue is a whopping **19 feet tall** (the tallest real woman ever recorded was only 8 feet 1¾ inches)!

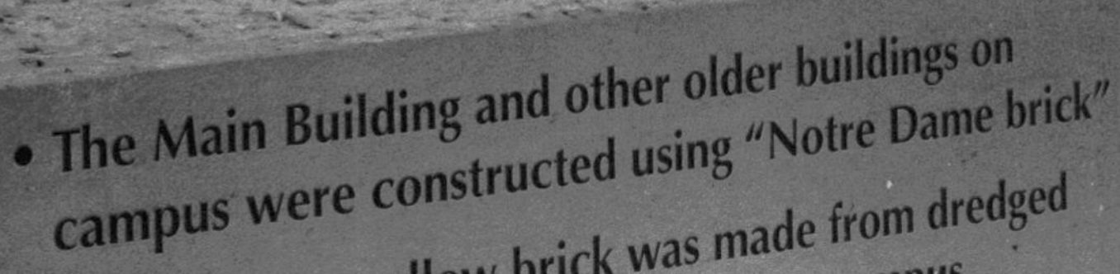

Did You Know...

There have been three Main Buildings on campus over the years?

- The first building was finished in 1849—more floors were later added above, but it was destroyed by a fire
- The second building was finished in 1865, but it was destroyed by a fire
- The third and current building was finished in 1879 and the Golden dome top was added in 1882

Building Credits

Architect: Willoughby J. Edbrooke (1843–1896)
Where He Lived: Chicago, Illinois

General Contractor: There wasn't one! The construction was supervised by Father Sorin (the founder of the University of Notre Dame) and other leaders at the time.

Can you spot the Golden Dome in this historical illustration?

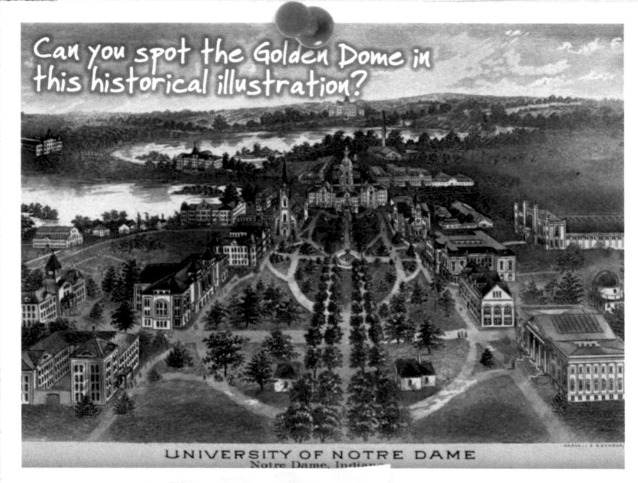

A Building of Many Uses

The building has been used for many different purposes over the years:

- classrooms
- dormitories
- administration offices
- general offices

Other Notable Historic Buildings on Campus:

- Washington Hall—1881
- LaFortune Student Center—1883
- Sorin Hall—1889

Campus Plan

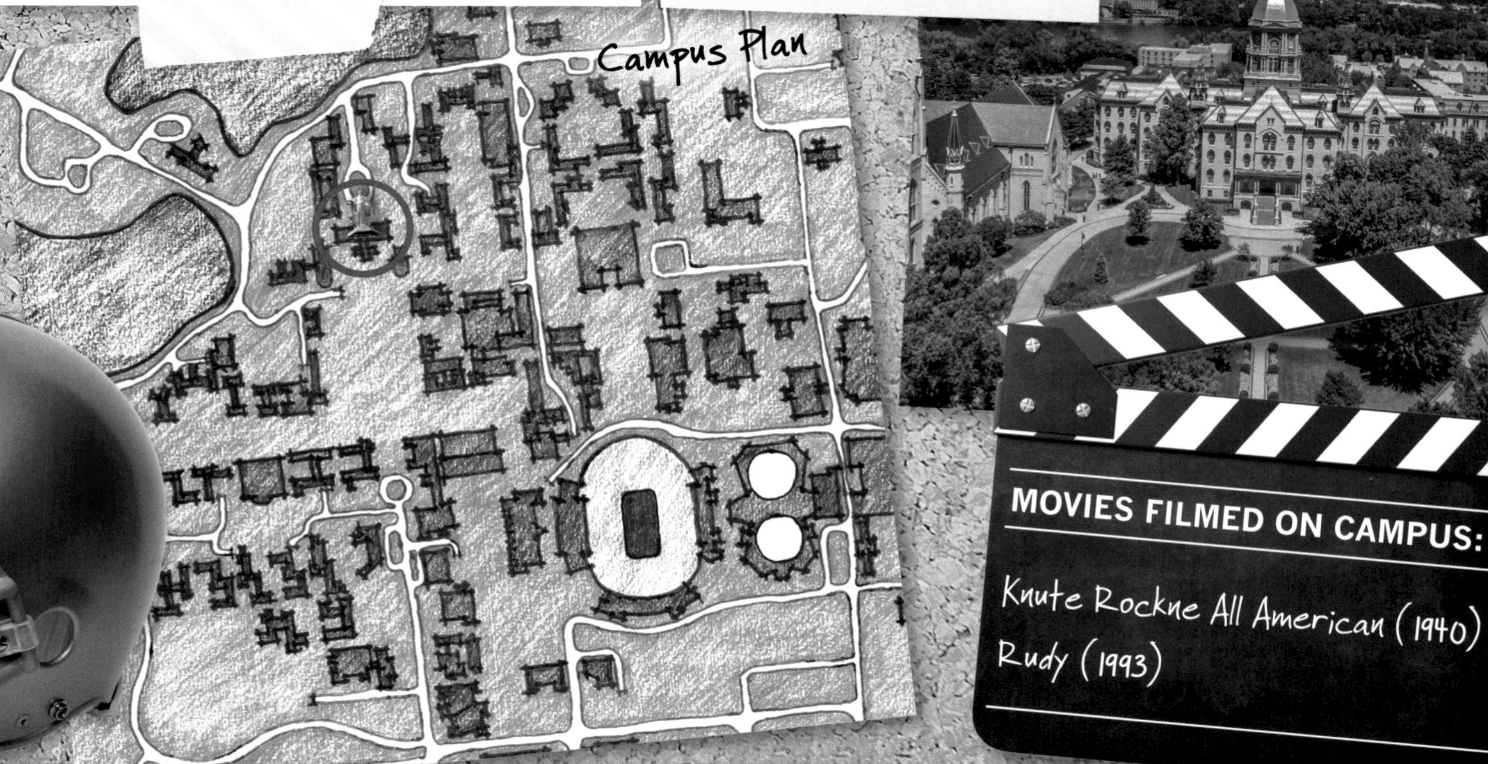

MOVIES FILMED ON CAMPUS:

Knute Rockne All American (1940)
Rudy (1993)

WEST BADEN SPRINGS HOTEL

FRENCH LICK, INDIANA

The building was completed on September 15th, 1902. It is one of the oldest hotels still open in Indiana. Following an extensive renovation, there was a grand reopening of the hotel in 2007.

THIS BUILDING IS IMPORTANT BECAUSE...

It is one of the oldest hotels still in operation in Indiana and is listed as a National Historic Landmark. The large freestanding dome was very innovative and unique when it was built, and the building has a long and storied history of its uses over the years.

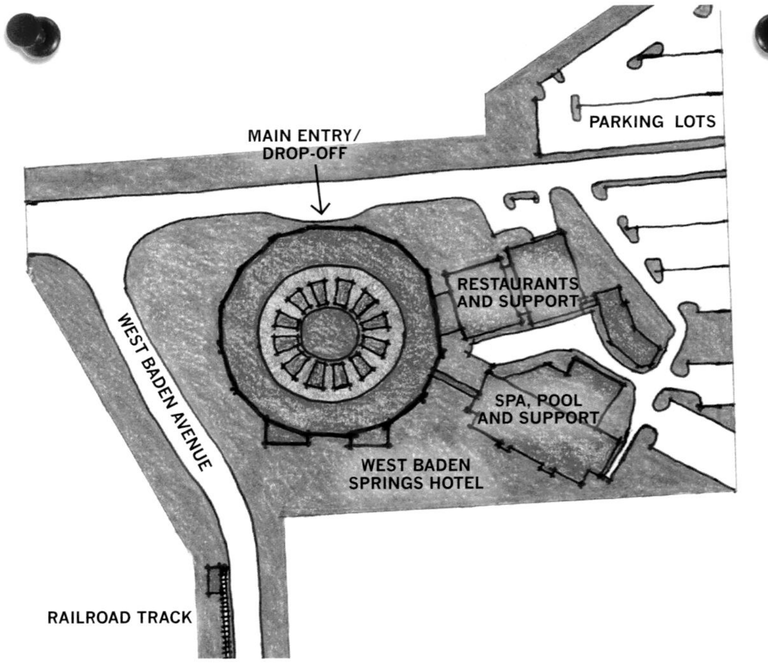

The dome that covers the atrium is 200 feet wide. This atrium was the largest free-span dome until the Houston Astrodome was constructed in the 1960s. This domed atrium was called the "8th Wonder of the World."

Houston Astrodome

DID YOU KNOW...

- The building was constructed in a fast track method
- A daily crew of 500 men worked 6 days a week to complete the project in about 270 days (that's about 9 months)!
- The hotel and property are located on 667 acres
- The trusses were custom designed for the large dome

Building Credits

Architect: Harrison Albright
Where He Lived: West Virginia

Structural Engineer: Oliver Wescott
He was a bridge engineer and designed the dome trusses

2007 Restoration and Renovation Architect:
George Ridgway—
Bloomington, Indiana

An Interesting History of Owners and Uses

1902 West Baden Springs Hotel opens
1929 Great Depression
1932 West Baden Springs Hotel closes
1934 Jesuits buy hotel. Jesuits open a seminary called West Baden College
1964 West Baden College closes
1966 Jesuits sell hotel to a Michigan couple who donate it to Northwood Institute (a private college)
1974 Property is listed as a National Historic Landmark
1985–1994 Property entangled in years of litigation for contested ownership
1996 Cook Group (Bloomington, Indiana) buys hotel and begins redevelopment
2007 West Baden Springs Hotel reopens

FRENCH LICK RESORT — WEST BADEN SPRINGS HOTEL

A train connects the West Baden Springs Hotel with the French Lick Springs Hotel! They are about 1.2 miles apart.

LIGHTS, CAMERA, ACTION!

The hotel was the setting for Michael Koryta's thriller "So Cold the River" in 2010.

BOONE COUNTY COURTHOUSE

LEBANON, INDIANA

Completed in 1911, it is one of 82 Indiana counties out of 92 that still have their original courthouse.

This building is important because...

- It is a fine example of a three-story classical revival-style building
- The primary building materials are granite and limestone from nearby Bedford, Indiana
- It features a beautiful art glass dome which is 52 feet in diameter—that makes it one of the largest courthouse domes in Indiana!
- It includes a clock tower above the large dome

One of the larger domes in the state belongs to none other than the West Baden Springs Hotel!

West Baden Springs Hotel

Did You Know...?

- A global meridian line runs right through the courthouse (thought to be the only public building in the world with this distinction!)
- This line is marked by a tablet consisting of a black and white marble arrow
- Four 35 foot tall Ionic style columns support a large pediment and porticoes. At the time they were built, these were the tallest solid stone columns in the United States

How can you tell this is an Ionic column? See those curvy designs at the top (called volutes)? That's how you'll know! Can you spot them on other buildings you see?

The Roman Numerals carved into the stone read "1909" for the year the building was begun, but the correct way to write that number in 2020 would be MCMIX!

Similar Projects by Joseph Hutton:

Newton County Courthouse—1906
Kentland, Indiana

Federal Judicial Center—1907
Hammond, Indiana

Lake County Federal Judicial Center—1907
Gary, Indiana

Federal Judicial Center—Addition—1941
Hammond, Indiana

Project Team:

Architect: Hutton & Hutton Architects and Engineers—Hammond, Indiana

Contractor: Caldwell & Drake—Columbus, Indiana

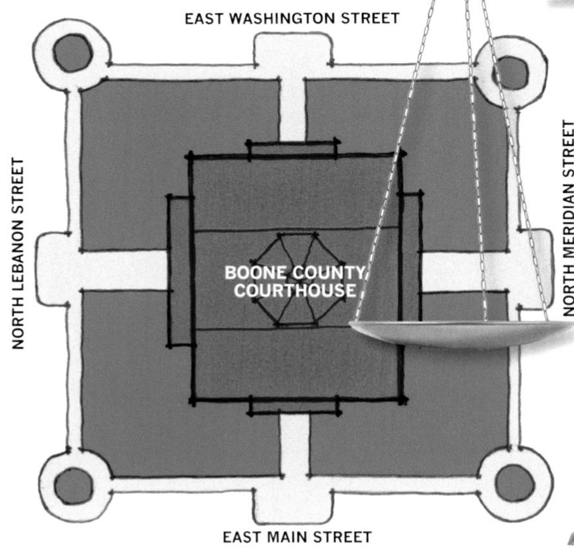

Who was Joseph T. Hutton?

Born in 1861, Hutton immigrated from Dunville, Canada. He received his architectural training from the University of Toronto and graduated in 1883 with a degree in architecture & engineering. Hutton & Hutton Architects and Engineers is still in existence today with a fifth generation owner, Justin Hutton.

LERNER THEATRE

ELKHART, INDIANA

This performing arts center was completed in 1924 during the Vaudeville era. The building was given a new life in 2011 with a complete return to its original grandeur (and name!) with an extensive project including demolition, renovation and new construction work.

THIS BUILDING IS IMPORTANT BECAUSE...

- The exterior design of the building is Beaux-Arts (Adams style)
- The exterior material of the building is terra cotta, which requires highly skilled artisans to construct
- There are very few buildings of this style and made of this material that remain in Indiana today

This portion of the building is an addition. Can you see where it begins? The addition looks like the original building!

Addition

Did You Know...?

- The project received an American Institute of Architects Indiana Honor Award in 2013
- The project received the Palladio Award in 2013 for Outstanding Achievement in Traditional Design
- The project received the Cook Cup for Outstanding Restoration of a project in Indiana

The building was designated as a National Historic Landmark in 1980. The theatre also contributes to the downtown Elkhart commercial historic district.

THE 2009 RENOVATION INCLUDED A NEW ADDITION:

- The restoration of this nearly 100 year old building included a new addition that changed the functionality of the building. It is unusual to have such an addition to a noteworthy historical building.
- The project design and budget were approved by the City of Elkhart in 2008
- The City of Elkhart approved an $18 million project budget
- Construction began in 2009 and was completed in 2011

Project Team: 2009 Renovation

Executive Architect: Cripe Design & Leedy/Cripe Architects—Elkhart, Indiana

Historic Preservation Architects: James T. Kienle Associates & Moody Nolan, Inc.—Indianapolis, Indiana

Interior Design: JJ Osterloo Design—Elkhart, Indiana

General Contractor: Majority Builders—South Bend, Indiana

PROJECT TEAM: ORIGINAL PROJECT

Architect: Vitzthum and Burns, Chicago, Illinois

Designer: Karl Martin Vitzthum (1880–1967)

This sign is part of the theatre's marquee. It's brightly lit and you can see lots of little lightbulbs at night.

LERNER

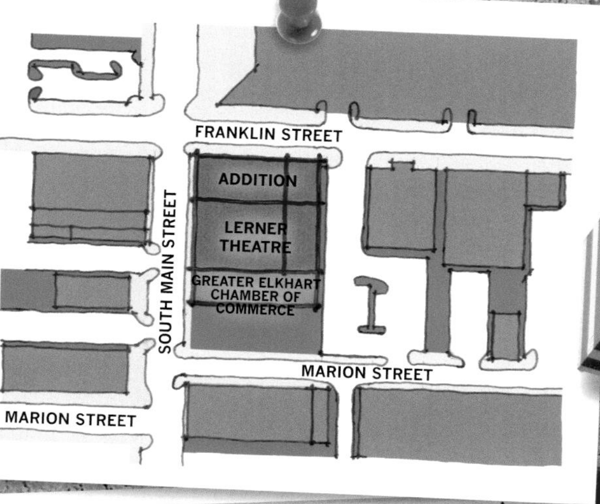

This is the architectural rendering drawn before the project was constructed

Do you think the actual building looks like this?

History of the Names, Uses, & Ownership

1924—Original Building

- The original owner was Henry Lerner
- First used as a Vaudeville theatre and evolved into a motion picture palace by the end of the 1920s

1931—Lerner sold the theatre to the Warner family

- The theatre was renamed, but the Warner family declared bankruptcy in 1933

1934—Illinois-Indiana Theatre aquired the Warner Theatre

- There was a county-wide contest to rename the theatre, which resulted in the new name, ELCO Theatre

1940—Theatre was aquired by the Manta and Rose Theatre chain

1961—Local businessman William Miller bought the theatre

1990—The Miller family sells the ELCO Theatre to a non-profit group called Premier Arts

1996—A matching fund grant was received from the National Endowment for the Arts

1997—The ELCO Commission for the Performing Arts was created

SAMARA

WEST LAFAYETTE, INDIANA

This single family residence is officially called the John and Catherine Christian House. It was designed by Frank Lloyd Wright and is one the finest examples of his Usonian style of design. It was completed in September 1956.

This Building is Important Because...

- It was one of the last homes designed by Frank Lloyd Wright and lived in by its original owner, the Christian Family
- It is designed in the Usonian Style of architecture which was the last design style used by Wright before his death
- Wright not only designed the house, but he designed all of the elements of the exterior and interior. Examples include: entrance gate, garden lanterns, furniture, fabrics, SAMARA logo/graphic design, piano hinges, door knobs, rugs, furniture, china, silverware, linens, bedspreads, table runners, lamps (and on and on!)
- Many of the interior design elements and furnishings were not originally produced but have since been added over the decades to make the home meet the true design vision of Wright
- It is now owned by the John Christian Family Memorial Trust, which protects and preserves the historic and significant home for decades to come

ABOUT THE ARCHITECT: FRANK LLOYD WRIGHT

- He was an American architect (1867–1959) educated at the University of Wisconsin—Madison
- He was also an interior designer, writer and educator
- He designed more than 1,000 buildings and structures
- Five hundred thirty-two of his plans were constructed and completed
- He created and designed for more than 70 years
- Wright believed in designing structures that are in harmony with humanity and the environment

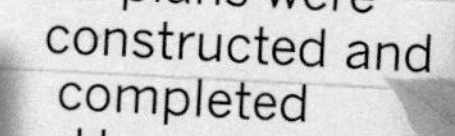

This furniture was also designed by Frank Lloyd Wright!

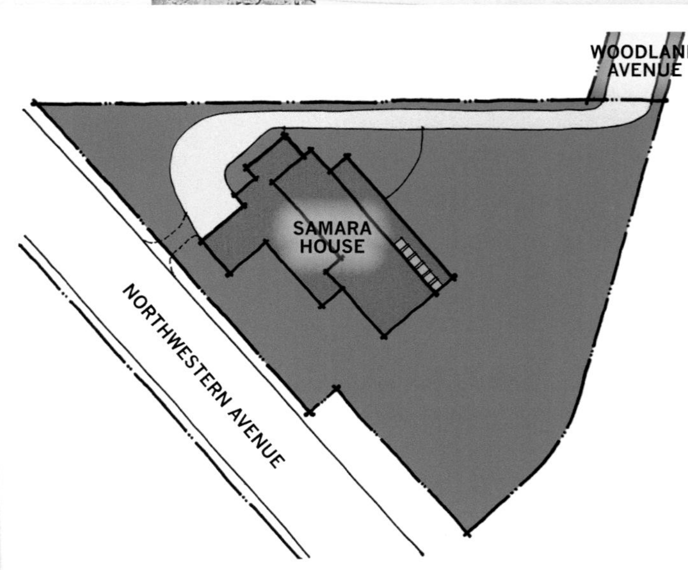

Did You Know...

- John and Catherine Christian commissioned Wright to design their dream home
- Frank Lloyd Wright named the residence SAMARA, for the "winged seeds found in pinecones" from the many pine trees nearby
- The last time the Christians met with Wright to discuss the design was on New Years Day of 1955
- The home was completed in 1956 and the Christians were the only family to live in SAMARA
- SAMARA is no longer occupied and is now available for public and private tours

DESIGN AND BUILDING CREDITS:

Assistant to Frank Lloyd Wright: Eugene Masselink

Architectural Apprentice & Brick Layer: Ed Kipta

Chief Carpenter & Furniture Maker: Evan Hinds

Exterior Framing & Interior Woodworking: Frank Woods

Construction Drawing Completion & on-site construction supervision: Ed Kipta

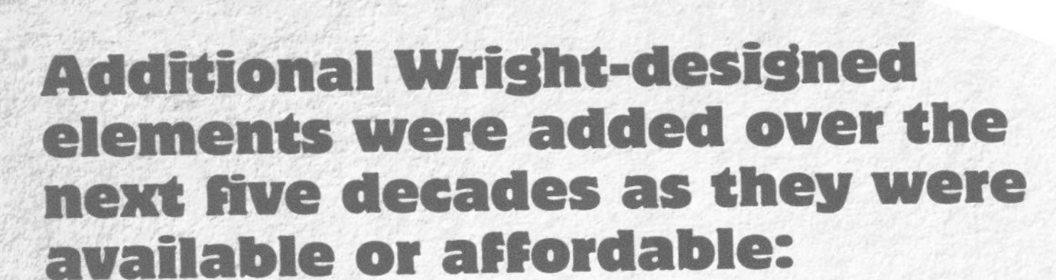

Additional Wright-designed elements were added over the next five decades as they were available or affordable:

1956 to 1959: Added landscaping, lanai brick wall, brick planter and entrance gate

1960's: Added paved brick driveway, oriental accessories, fascia boards with SAMARA logo and air conditioning

1970's and 1980's: Added copper garden lanterns, dining table, dining chairs, lanai furniture and the light post at the driveway

1990's: Added built-in cabinet for television, ornamental copper fascia, light poles for the carport, table lamps for the guest bedroom, SAMARA rug for living room, SAMARA vase, outdoor planters and a floor lamp

2000's: Added living room floor lamp with oriental shade, accent table lamp with rice paper shade, origami chair and SAMARA bedspreads

Usonion Style...what's that?

Primary elements of this style include:

- Integrating the house with the site and nature
- A masonry mass on stone and concrete footings with a fireplace core
- Large window screens of quarter-inch plate glass
- Two flat roofs with wide overhangs
- Concrete slab floor with pipes embedded for gravity heat

EMENS AUDITORIUM AND MUSIC COMPLEX

BALL STATE UNIVERSITY • MUNCIE, INDIANA

Construction on the original building was started in 1961 and completed in 1964.

THIS BUILDING IS IMPORTANT BECAUSE:

The design and building have stood the test of time and even with changes over the years, the auditorium still has great acoustics—the sound quality is just as good today as it was during the very first performance.

The building is located at the heart of the school campus, and is the centerpiece of a cultural complex that includes Hargreaves Music Building, Arts and Communications Building and Pruis Hall.

This is what the building looked like when it opened

Have you ever attended a live musical performace?

Meet the Building Namesake: University President John Emens

He was the 6th president of Ball State University, from 1945 to 1968 (23 years). His goal was to create a campus of the future, and he wanted to provide arts, cultural events and musical performances for Ball State, Muncie and Eastern Indiana.

Did You Know...

- The stage is 144 feet wide and 45 feet deep. That's half of a football field in both directions!
- From the stage floor to the steel above is 78 feet, which is as tall as a 7 to 8 story building.
- The main stage curtain weighs 16 tons. That's equal to the weight of 3 African elephants!
- The proscenium arch is 82 feet wide, which could fit 3 double decker London buses end to end.

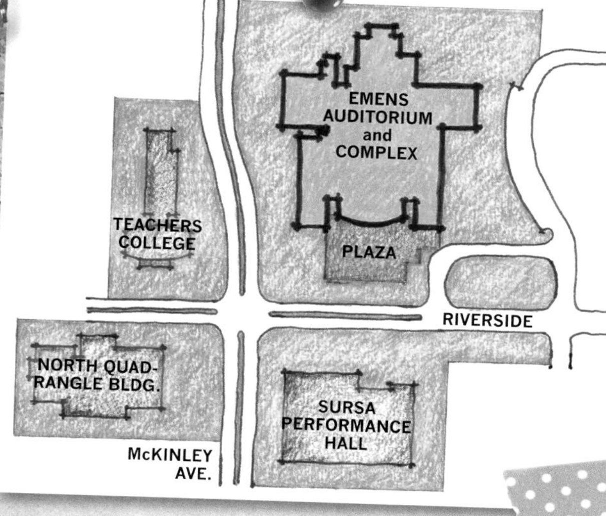

Architect and Project Team

Original Building

Architect: Scholer and Associates—West Lafayette, Indiana

General Contractor: Hagerman Construction—Ft. Wayne, Indiana

2018 Addition and Renovation

Architect: MSKTD and Associates—Ft. Wayne, Indiana

General Contractor: Pridemark Construction—Muncie, Indiana

Additional Projects and Improvements Since the Building Opened

1995: Minor renovation and interior refresh

2005: Minor renovation and interior refresh

2017: New hospitality suite and exterior balcony added, updated ADA restrooms and entryways, and other public space improvements

2018: Phase 1 East Mall—hardscape additions which included a car drop off, two limestone sculptures and a forecourt for the East Mall

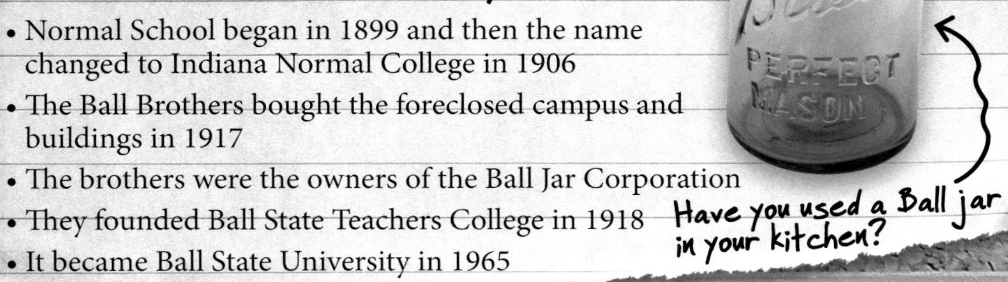

About Ball State University

- Normal School began in 1899 and then the name changed to Indiana Normal College in 1906
- The Ball Brothers bought the foreclosed campus and buildings in 1917
- The brothers were the owners of the Ball Jar Corporation
- They founded Ball State Teachers College in 1918
- It became Ball State University in 1965

Have you used a Ball jar in your kitchen?

Emens Auditorium
3,581 seats

Pruis Hall
410 seats
(part of Emens complex)

AUDITORIUM SEATING CAPACITY

THE REPUBLIC BUILDING

COLUMBUS, INDIANA

Completed in 1971, it was originally a newspaper building—the office and printing press for The Republic newspaper. As of 2018, it now houses the Indiana University J. Irwin Miller Architecture Program.

DID YOU KNOW...

Columbus has over 80 architecturally significant buildings designed by famous and important architects.

Rows of trees that are side by side and lined up exactly are known as an "allée of trees".

This was the trademark landscape design feature of Dan Kiley in many of his Columbus, Indiana landscapes.

You can see the allée of trees right here

THE BUILDING WAS LISTED ON THE NATIONAL REGISTER OF HISTORIC PLACES AND DESIGNATED AS A NATIONAL HISTORIC LANDMARK IN 2012.

The printing process on display (from 1971 to 1997)

The simple mid-century building with floor to ceiling glass windows was specially designed to put on full display all of the work and activities related to the creation and printing of a newspaper. The bright yellow printing press that could be seen from 2nd Street and the nearby sidewalks was a real highlight to all who passed.

printing press

office space

These two photos show the building in use with the printing press and later, as office space

This building is important because:

- It was listed as a National Historic Landmark in 2012
- It received a national AIA Honor Award in 1975
- It was one of first buildings to use moveable partitions, or dividers, for work stations
- It was one of first buildings to be constructed in downtown following the Columbus urban renewal program
- It is part of Columbus's architecturally significant buildings and landscapes program
- It is an early adopter of using the lean/six sigma process for operations (an efficiency process system)

Building Credits:

Architect: Skidmore Owings Merrill—Chicago, Illinois

Designer: Myron Goldsmith

Landscape Architect: Dan Kiley—Charlotte, Vermont

Interior Design: Skidmore Owings Merrill—Chicago, Illinois

General Contractor: Dunlap & Company—Columbus, Indiana

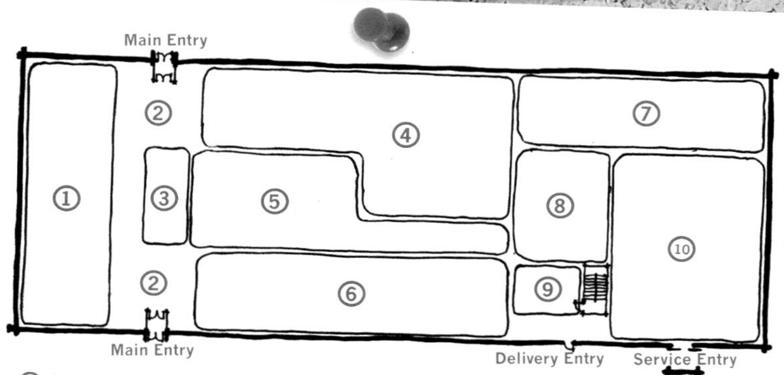

① Administration Team & Support
② Lobby
③ Restrooms
④ Advertising & Composing Team Support
⑤ Team Offices Support Area
⑥ Editorial & Circulation Teams Area
⑦ Printing Press
⑧ Paper Printing Preparation
⑨ Truck Driver Support
⑩ Paper Distribution & Support Team
⑪ Service Elevator

FIRST FLOOR PLAN CONCEPT DIAGRAM

EXTRA! EXTRA! The Newspaper is on the Move

In 1997, the Republic Newspaper relocated the newspaper printing and related functions to the Printing Center—an architecturally significant building located along Interstate 65.

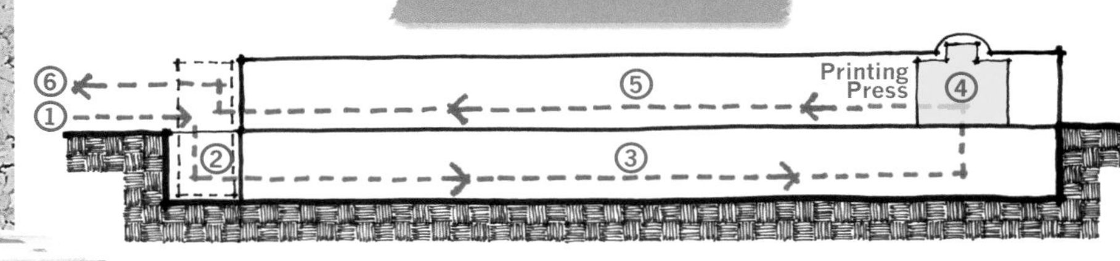

① Raw paper is unloaded from trucks
② Raw paper goes down an exterior elevator
③ Raw paper is prepared for the printing press
④ The newspaper is printed
⑤ The newspaper is prepared for delivery
⑥ The newspaper is loaded on trucks for delivery

BUILDING CROSS SECTION

RAW PAPER TO PRINTING TO NEWSPAPER DELIVERY FLOW

SIMON SKJODT ASSEMBLY HALL

INDIANA UNIVERSITY (I.U.) • BLOOMINGTON, INDIANA

Construction of the building started in 1969 and was finished in 1971.

THIS BUILDING IS IMPORTANT BECAUSE:

It's the home of the I.U. Basketball Team and the on-campus location for students and faculty to walk to watch basketball games, concerts, entertainment and other events. I.U. National Championship banners hang from the ceiling for all to see:

1940 • 1953 • 1976
1981 • 1987

DID YOU KNOW...

- The first Assembly Hall was called Men's Gym
  - It was used from 1901 to 1917
  - It had seating for 600
  - It hosted the Indiana High School Basketball Championships
- Since 1971, over **6 MILLION** fans have attended men's basketball games in the current Assembly Hall!

HOME COURT ADVANTAGE: MEMORABLE BASKETBALL GAMES

- **December 20th, 1971:** Building Dedication Game, I.U. beats Notre Dame: 91–27
- **2001:** I.U. beats #1 ranked Michigan State University
- **2011:** I.U. beats #1 ranked University of Kentucky
- **2011:** I.U. beats #2 ranked Ohio State University

This was the first game in Assembly Hall!

Architect and Project Team

Architect: Eggers & Higgins—New York, New York

Structural Engineer: Severud Associates—New York, New York

General Contractor: F.A. Wilhelm Construction—Indianapolis, Indiana

Additional Projects and Improvements Since Assembly Hall Opened:

1995: New floor and seating improvements
2005: Scoreboard/videoboard added
2010: New Cook Hall added next door
2016: Significant renovation and improvements. Renamed to Simon Skjodt Assembly Hall

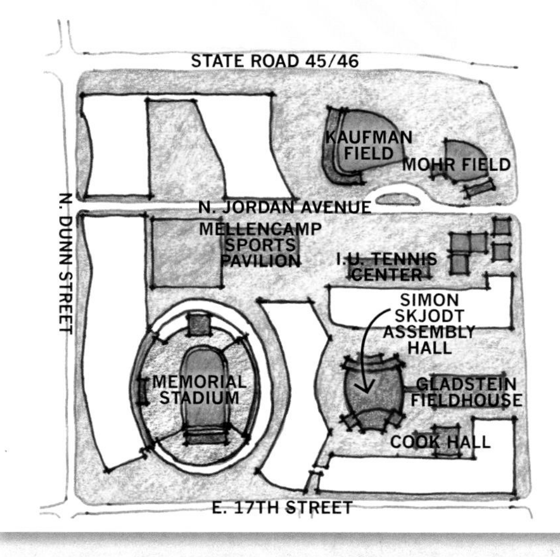

Eggers & Higgins—I.U. Architect

- Otto Eggers designed the majority of the on-campus projects from 1941 to 1971.
- His significant projects include:
  - Fine Arts Building
  - Lilly Library
  - Football Stadium
  - Eigenmann Hall
  - Briscoe Hall
  - Forest Hall
  - Wilkie Hall

More About Assembly Hall:

The 2016 renovation included all new seats. The seating in the Henke Spirit of 76 Club is 40 feet above the basketball floor! Speaking of the new floor, it is made of maple wood from Indiana trees. The new scoreboard is 31.2 feet by 17.7 feet (this is slightly bigger than 3 dorm rooms!).

ARTS UNITED CENTER

FORT WAYNE, INDIANA

This building includes an auditorium with two separate rehearsal halls. It also acts as a center for education, classes and exhibits of the arts. It was completed in 1973.

THIS BUILDING IS IMPORTANT BECAUSE:

- It is located in downtown Fort Wayne and contributes to the urban fabric of the city
- It is the only building designed by Louis Kahn in Indiana and the Midwest
- Louis Kahn is a nationally and internationally known architect
- It gives lots of people in Ft. Wayne (and beyond) the chance to see many cultural arts performances

This is the architect's sketch of the exterior design. Can you spot the changes to the real building?

What would you say about the building if someone asked?

"I asked the brick what it wanted to be... and it wanted to be an arch"
-Louis Kahn

"Kahn wrapped ruins around his buildings"
-Architecture critic

Louis Kahn featured the following design concepts in this building:

- A plain and simple exterior of brick and concrete surrounds the theatre inside
- The building is almost completely plain on the outside. It is made up of simple geometric shapes—circles, triangles, and arches—to add some interest
- The entrance has shallow, arched windows that illuminate the inside with the sunlight that shines through
- Every seat in the auditorium has a clear view of the bottom middle of the house curtain
- For great sound quality (called the "acoustics") during performances, the materials used include brick, concrete and plenty of oak wood

Did You Know...

- The main performance auditorium is shared by the Civic Theatre, Youth Theatre, Ballet, Dance Collective and Philharmonic. That's a lot of different uses!
- The rest of the building is a community resource for gallery space, meetings, lectures, receptions and public rentals
- It includes two soundproof rehearsal halls as big as the main stage

BUILDING CREDITS

Architect: Louis Kahn (1901–1974)
Where he was born: Parnü, Russia (now Estonia)
Where he lived: New Haven, Connecticut

Louis Kahn, whom at the time he died, was thought by some to be the best architect in America during his career

DID YOU KNOW (LOUIS KAHN EDITION)...

- He went to college at the University of Pennsylvania School of Design and graduated in 1924
- He was a Professor of Architecture at the Yale School of Architecture for 10 years (1947–1957)
- He was a Professor of Architecture at the University of Pennsylvania School of Design for 16 years (1957–1973)
- He received the AIA Gold Medal Award, which is the institute's highest individual honor, in 1973

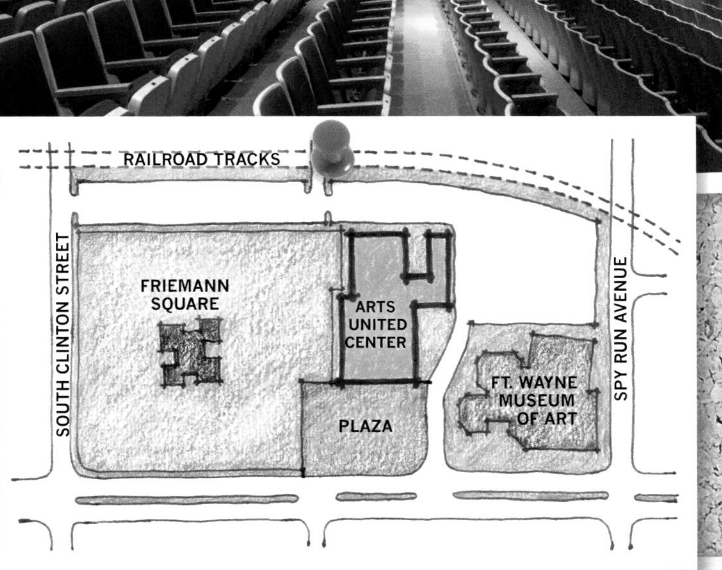

HOW MANY PEOPLE CAN FIT INSIDE?

- The main auditorium has 660 seats
- The second floor gallery has 100-150 seats and standing room for 250-300 people

That's a grand total of 1,010–1,110 people in the building at one time!

And The Award Goes To...

Kahn designed five buildings that earned the prestigious 25 Year Building Award given by the American Institute of Architects. Here they are, in no particular order:

1. Salk Institute for Biological Studies in La Jolla, California (1992)
2. Yale University Art Gallery in New Haven, Connecticut (1979)
3. Kimball Museum of Art in Ft. Worth, Texas (1998)
4. Phillips Exeter Academy Library in Exeter, New Hampshire (1997)
5. Yale Center for British Art in New Haven, Connecticut (2005)

CHILDREN'S MUSEUM OF INDIANAPOLIS

INDIANAPOLIS, INDIANA

The original building was completed in 1976 and is the largest children's museum in the world!

This building is important because...

The museum has consistently been ranked as one of the best in the United States with many hands-on exhibits for kids, both young and old. The exhibit team is known world-wide for its research and development of exhibits. They consult with subject experts to provide the best and most authentic exhibits to the museum.

The museum is very popular and has over **1 MILLION** visitors every year!

There are exciting and fun holiday and special events that happen at the museum throughout the year:

- **Christmas season:** two-story "snow" slide in the main lobby for kids of all ages
- **Halloween:** haunted house

Seymour and Riad, the massive dinosaurs seen "breaking in" to the museum are brachiosaurs!

- A Cinedome was added in 1996 to provided an unique experience for 310 museum-goers at a time.
- In 2004, the Cinedome was converted to a Dinosphere, which was built within and around the Cinedome.

The museum has a working carousel in the building

Did You Know...

In the lobby of the original building there is a winding ramp for visitors to easily walk from floor to floor. In the middle is an atrium with **"Fireworks of Glass"**—a huge, five-story tall glass sculpture by Dale Chihuly that was installed in 2006.

Building Credits

1976—Original Building
Architect: Wright Porteus & Lowe
Indianapolis, Indiana

1988—Major Addition
Architect: Woolen Molzan & Partners
Indianapolis, Indiana

2009—Major Addition
Architect: Ratio Architects
Indianapolis, Indiana

General Contractor:
Shiel Sexton
Indianapolis, Indiana

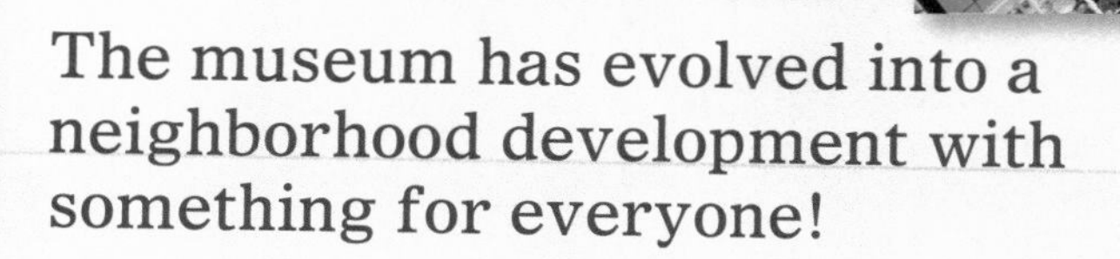

The museum has evolved into a neighborhood development with something for everyone!

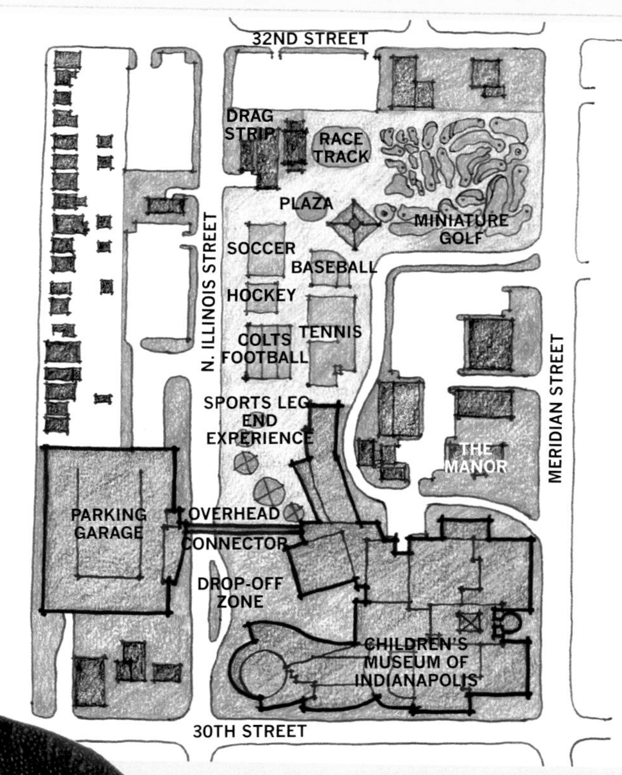

The Riley Children's Health Sports Legend Experience was finished in 2018 and gives visitors a chance to explore in the 7.5 acre interactive playground. Some of the Indiana-themed elements include:

- Pete & Alice Dye Golf Experience—27 hole miniature golf course
- Indianapolis Motor Speedway pedal car racetrack
- Indy Fuel mini ice hockey rink
- And many others

FALLS OF THE OHIO INTERPRETIVE CENTER

CLARKSVILLE, INDIANA

The Interpretive Center is located within a state park on the north banks of the Ohio River and provides direct access to the world's most accessible Devonian fossil beds. The building was completed in 1994.

THIS HISTORIC SITE AND BUILDING ARE IMPORTANT BECAUSE:

- It is located where Lewis & Clark met to begin their historic western expedition to the Continental Divide and on to the Pacific Ocean in 1803
- The lower falls of the Ohio River in the park reveal the worlds largest Devonian fossil beds which are 390 million years old
- The center informs visitors about the history of the Falls of the Ohio and provides direct access to the northern bank of the Ohio River

Did You Know...?

- The McAlpine Locks and Dam reveal the Devonian fossil beds which are visible primarily in the summer and fall when they are not covered by river water
- Prior to the opening of the Interpretive Center, visitors would park on the road along the river and climb down the river bank to experience the falls and Devonian fossil beds
- The Ohio River elevation change at the Louisville falls is 37 feet, which is the tallest waterfall within the entire Ohio River system

Fossil example

Original Building Design Concepts:

- It acts as a hands-on science museum for children that spans 390 million years of natural and cultural history
- It educates the community and inspires newfound curiosity about the region's past
- It provides an outdoor experience from the Center, directly to the fossil beds & Ohio River. In addition, adjacent trails can be used to explore historic paths
- It has an immersive interior media experience centered on the Lewis and Clark Expedition into the Pacific Northwest

Can you spot these design themes?

- Mixed material "rock-like" layered exterior
- Triangular design element welcoming visitors inside
- Circular atrium
- Rounded windows for expansive views
- Building placement in proximity to the river bank

Project Team: Original Building

Architect and Civil Engineer: Woolpert & Associates—Dayton, Ohio

General Contractor: Sullivan & Cozart—Louisville, Kentucky

Project Team: New Exhibits and Interior Updates

Architect: Barnett Bagley Architects, PSC—Lexington, Kentucky

Structural Engineer: Poage Engineers & Associates, Inc.—Lexington, Kentucky

Consulting Engineer: Shrout Tate Wilson Consulting Engineers—Louisville, Kentucky

Exposed fossils in the Ohio River bed

WHITE CHAPEL

ROSE-HULMAN INSTITUTE OF TECHNOLOGY
TERRE HAUTE, INDIANA

This chapel, completed in 2001, is a non-denominational place of worship and contemplation located on the campus of Rose-Hulman Institute.

THIS BUILDING IS IMPORTANT BECAUSE:

- It is located on a prominent site overlooking a small lake
- It provides a significant multi-functional space on campus that is used in many different ways
- It is an iconic building on a campus full of academic buildings

Uses of the Building:

- Worship and contemplation
- Weddings and wedding receptions
- Rose-Hulman Institute events
- Community events
- Informal gatherings and events

HELLO
my name is

The formal name of the building is the

John R. and Elizabeth L. White Chapel at Rose-Hulman Institute

It was named for John White who is a supportive and generous Rose-Hulman Institute graduate and a local Terre Haute businessman. Quite a mouthful!

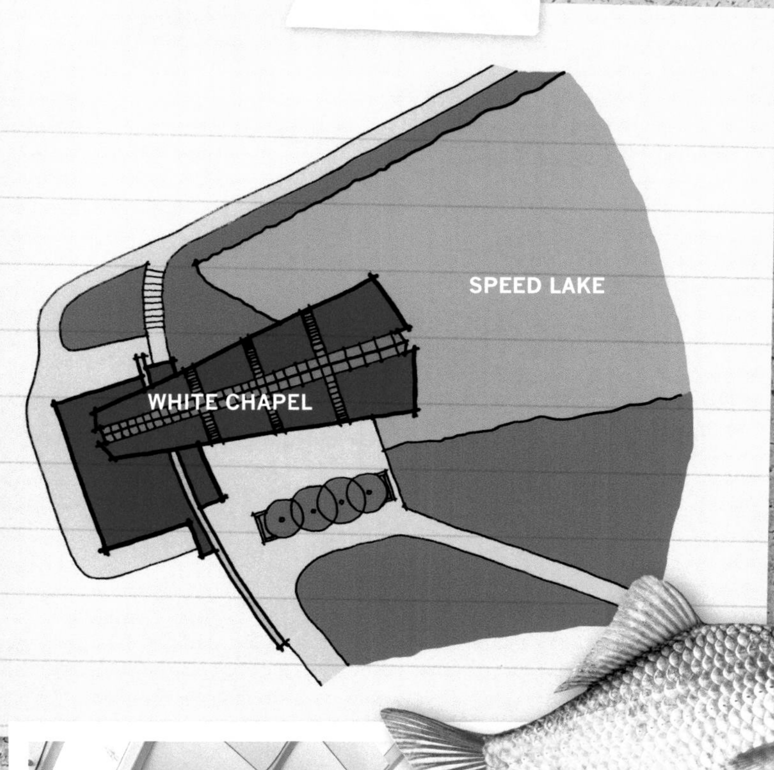

Project Team

Architect: VOA Associates—Chicago, Illinois
Lead designer—William Ketchum

Exterior Architect: Zahner—Kansas City, Missouri (roof, wall and glazing systems)

An Unusual Exterior Shape and Material

The exterior of the building is made up of silver colored diamond-shaped stainless steel shingles

- The exterior design shape required a custom-engineered design innovation
- The exterior "skin" material expands and contracts as the surface heats up in the summer and cools in the winter
- The custom-fabricated shingles are made to exact specifications through the use of robotics and customized automated methods

And The Award Goes To...

The project has received several design awards, including:

1. AIA Chicago 2015 Design Excellence—Interior Architecture Award
2. Citation of Merit—Divine Detail Award

Kid Architect

LUCAS OIL STADIUM

INDIANAPOLIS, INDIANA

This building took almost 3 years to construct. It was started in September 2005 and finished in August 2008. It is both a sports stadium and venue for other large events.

The roof is retractable which can be left either open or closed

- The roof takes between 9 and 11 minutes to open or close
- The roof opening is 300 feet by 588 feet in size. That's the size of 6 football fields!

You can see the open window and open roof here!

THE MOVEABLE WINDOW OPENS FOR VIEW OF THE SOLDIERS & SAILORS MONUMENT ON THE CIRCLE

- The open window can be seen from the majority of the seats in the stadium
- The window opening is 244 feet x 88 feet. That's the size of a whole football field!

Lucas Oil Stadium is known as "The House that Peyton Manning built" (Colts QB from 1998 to 2011)

CONSTRUCTION BY THE NUMBERS...

130,000
cubic yards of cast-in-place concrete

16,000
tons of steel

That's about the same weight as 2,600 elephants!

9,100
glass windows

1,440
pieces of architectural precast (exterior material for buildings)

700
pieces of structural precast concrete

This building is important because:

- It is located in downtown Indianapolis
- The stadium is used for sports and athletic events of all kinds:
  Indianapolis Colts Football • Indy Eleven Soccer • NCAA Basketball Tournament • College and High School Football
- The stadium is used for other local and national events:
  Conventions • National Competitions for Bands and Drum Corps • Concerts

Building Credits

Architect: HKS Architects—Dallas, Texas

Associate Architects: Browning Day Mullins Dierdorf—Indianapolis, Indiana
A2SO4—Indianapolis, Indiana

Consulting Engineer: Moore Engineers—Houston, Texas

General Contractors: Hunt Construction Group—Indianapolis, Indiana
Smoot Construction—Indianapolis, Indiana
Mezzetta Construction—Indianapolis, Indiana

Tours of Lucas Oil Stadium can be scheduled at the stadium website: www.lucasoilstadium.com

STADIUM CAPACITY

Seating capacity for Colts games is 67,000 fans. This makes Lucas Oil Stadium the 12th largest city in Indiana during games!

At the peak of construction, there were eleven construction cranes on the site. Can you spot them all?

EVANSVILLE MUSEUM OF ARTS, HISTORY & SCIENCE EYKAMP PAVILION ADDITION

EVANSVILLE, INDIANA

Completed in 2014, this new addition to the existing museum includes a new entrance and the Koch Immersive Theater.

THIS BUILDING IS IMPORTANT BECAUSE:

- It is located on an important downtown public site on the banks of the Ohio River
- It includes a state-of-the-art immersive domed theatre with 360° digital projection built within the building "box"
- It redefines the main building entrance

DESIGN CONCEPT:

- The new pavilion is a simple white terra cotta "box" positioned in front of the existing museum to welcome visitors over a new, reimagined plaza
- This pavilion serves as a window into the museum and its three core disciplines: arts, history, and science
- The white box serves as a canvas to highlight the composition and positioning of the dome theater and gallery components

Did You Know...

- The exterior of the addition is clad with architectural terra cotta. This is a glazed masonry building material created from molded clay.
- The museum was closed for about a year during the key construction phase and re-opened to the public on February 7, 2014.

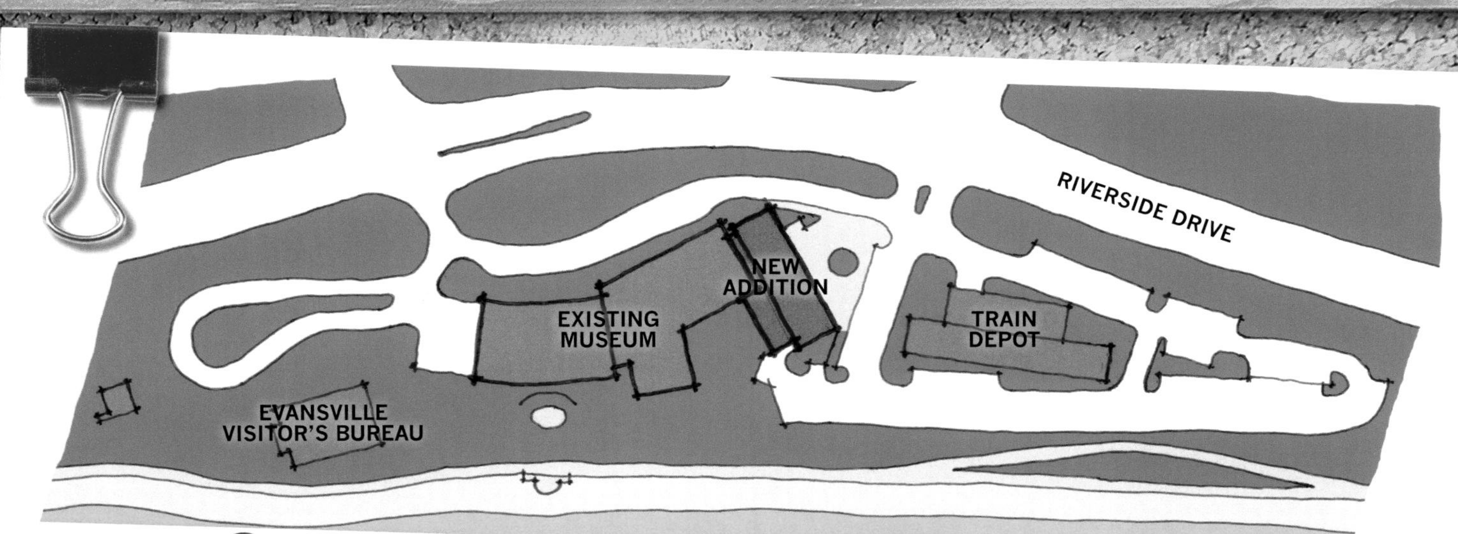

Building Credits—Eykamp Pavilion Addition

Design Architect: Ratio Architects, Inc.
Indianapolis, Indiana

Architect of Record: VPS Architecture
Evansville, Indiana

Project One Studio designed, fabricated and installed the two imaginative artistic elements:

1. Custom milled acrylic glass paneling for the new staircase and balcony
2. Custom cut wood cladding on the immersive theater dome

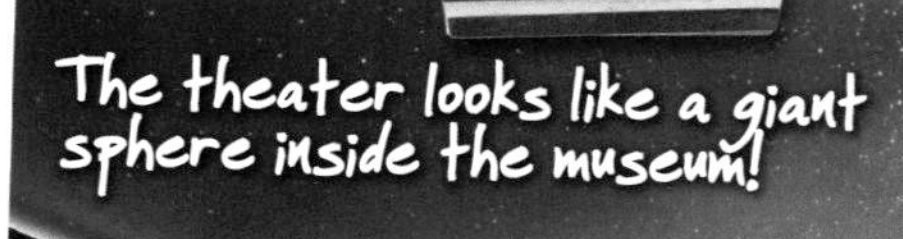

And The Award Goes To...

The Eykamp Pavilion addition has received some awards for it's design:

1. 2014 Merit Award—Indiana Chapter of the American Institute of Architects
2. 2015 Interior Design Excellence Award—IIDA (International Interior Design Association)

WILMETH ACTIVE LEARNING CENTER

PURDUE UNIVERSITY • WEST LAFAYETTE, INDIANA

This building was completed in August 2017 on the site of the old Heating and Power Plant North.

This Building is Important Because:

It provides students of the university with an ideal environment for a new way of learning. It combined two engineering libraries into one common library, and it is located at the center of campus for easy access by many students.

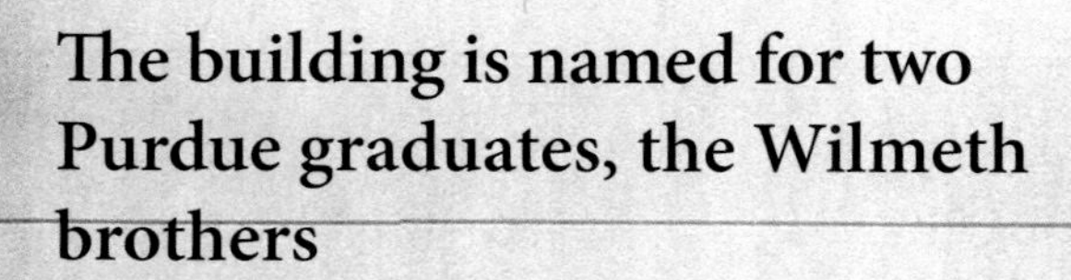

The building is named for two Purdue graduates, the Wilmeth brothers

- Thomas Wilmeth graduated in 1935 with a degree in Electrical Engineering
- Harvey Wilmeth graduated in 1940 with a degree in Chemical Engineering
- Their family founded Scot Industries which is located in Milwaukee, Wisconsin
- Scot Industries provides products for the hydraulic and cylinder markets

The building is located on the former heat & power plant site (originally built in 1924) and the Engineering Administration Building

DID YOU KNOW...

- The learning center is located at the center of the campus
- There can be 5,000 students and faculty in the building at one time
- Purdue University has one of the largest engineering schools in the country
- Purdue University has more graduates who are astronauts and have traveled into space than any other university

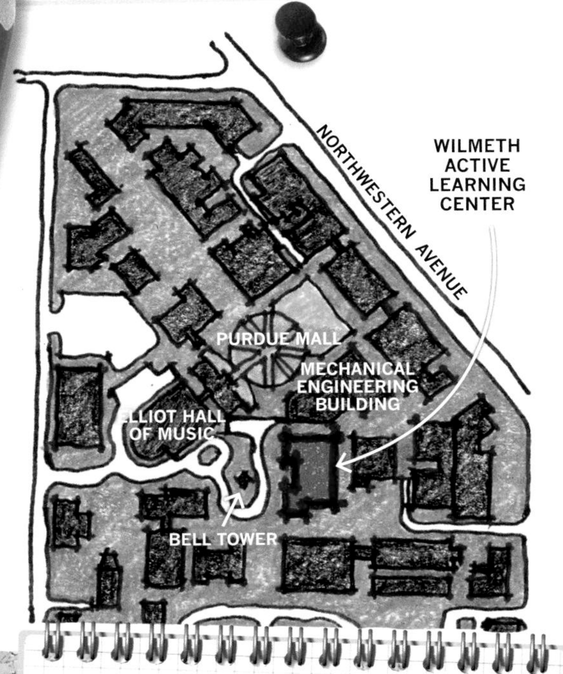

The previous library model has now become active learning centers' new classroom type and model:

- Professors do not stand in the front of the class and lecture
- Students sit in groups at tables for collaboration and discussions
- Students retain more of the information with this model instead of from listening to lectures and memorizing facts
- Students participate in the teaching and leading of the class

CAPACITY BY THE NUMBERS

5,000 students can be accommodated at one time

27 groupings of active learning classrooms and collaboration rooms with adjacent library spaces

1 small auditorium that is available to the entire university

Building Credits

Architect: BSA LifeStructures—Indianapolis, Indiana

Landscape Architect: BSA LifeStructures—Indianapolis, Indiana

General Contractors: F.A. Wilhelm Construction—Indianapolis, Indiana
Turner Construction—Indianapolis, Indiana

Demolition of the former power plant

- The power plant opened in 1924
- It included a 250 foot high smoke stack which was an iconic landmark for many decades until the 1990s, **seen in the drawing to the left.**

These are some of the old power plant parts!

The new building took inspiration from the former power plant with:

- A massive open four story stairwell
- Exposed structural trusses with large openings
- Reclaimed artifacts used in new building include:
  water pumps • catwalk grates • oversized brick • turbines • wheels • gauges • boiler hatches • ash cart

PUBLIC ART: "LOVE"

LOCATED AT NEWFIELDS (FORMERLY THE INDIANAPOLIS MUSEUM OF ART)

Created in 1970 by artist Robert Indiana, this iconic pop art image and sculpture became a national and international success.

The steel has additives that cause it to have a rusted look at Newfields Museum

SCULPTURE FAST FACTS:

- The typeface of the sculpture is Didone Bold
- Since the original sculpture was made, Robert Indiana created 50 more "Love" sculptures of different sizes and materials

AN ICON WITH AN INTERESTING HISTORY:

Robert Indiana first created the "LOVE" 2-dimensional image for the 1965 Museum of Modern Art (NYC) Christmas card. This image became the basis of the first "LOVE" sculpture which was located at the Indianapolis Museum of Art. In 1973, the United States Postal Service created the LOVE stamp which was a huge success (300 million stamps were issued!)

A postage stamp only cost 8¢ back in 1973... do you know how much they cost today?

ABOUT THE ARTIST: ROBERT INDIANA (1928–2018)

- He was born Robert Clark and grew up in New Castle, Indiana
- Educated at the Herron School of Art & Design (Indianapolis)
- Indiana moved to New York City in 1956 and quickly became a reputable artist and early leader in the Pop Art movement
- He was a painter, sculptor and printmaker who was known for his work in advancing Pop Art

The sculpture used to be outside, now it's located indoors

Have you spotted any artwork or sculptures outside near where you live?

PUBLIC ART: "ENGINEERING FOUNTAIN"

LOCATED ON THE PURDUE UNIVERSITY MALL IN WEST LAFAYETTE

This Sculpture is Important Because...

It was a gift from the Class of 1939 to honor their 50 year reunion and graduation from Purdue. The College of Engineering is important at Purdue and is one of the largest engineering colleges in the country.

Engineering Stats

- Includes four vertical parabolic structures with a large jet of water spraying up through the center
- A mirrored steel cylinder was later added around the water jet for safety reasons
- Contains 228 tons of concrete
- There is no fence to keep visitors out of the fountain
- The water drains through a metal grate in the ground as there is no pool to collect it
- Cost $350,000 to build in 1989

ABOUT THE DESIGN TEAM:

- Artist Robert Youngman was a Professor at the University of Illinois
- He designed a large number of concrete sculptures between 1962 and 1995
- Youngman's daughter, Taresah Youngman, assisted in the project
- The lighting design was done by Jones & Phillips Associates of Memphis, Tennessee

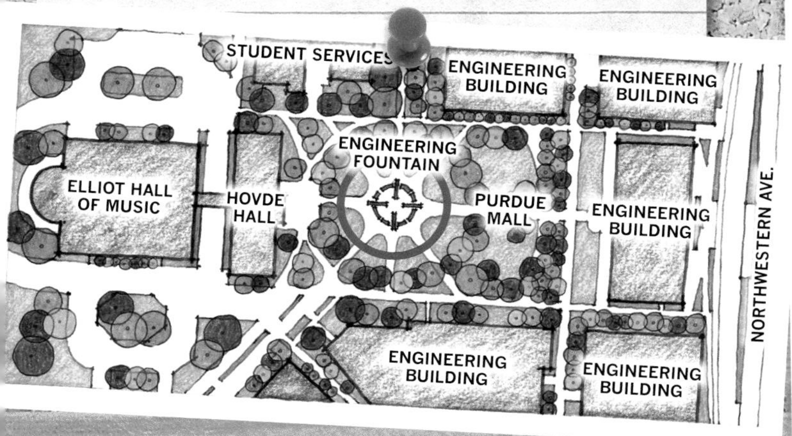

Did You Know...

- The Purdue Mall is often referred to as the Engineering Mall due to the proximity of engineering buildings surrounding it
- The sculpture and water feature are also known as the "Class of 1939 Water Sculpture"
- An original napkin sketch of the sculpture was discussed by Youngman and the Department Head of the Creative Arts over coffee at the Memorial Union Building
- A 20 minute light show runs every night from April to October

PUBLIC ART: "CONVERGENCE"

LOCATED IN PROMENADE PARK IN FT. WAYNE

About Promenade Park:

"Convergence" is the first public art sculpture to be included at Promenade Park, a new public park at the confluence of the Maumee, St. Joseph and St. Mary Rivers. The goal of this new park is to "make the rivers an active part of our community" according to Mayor Tom Henry.

The sculpture is located in the southeast corner of the park, at the intersection of Superior & Harrison Streets.

About the Sculpture:

- A competition of 5 nationally known artists was sponsored by the City of Ft. Wayne
- The competition jury unanimously selected "Convergence" as the winning design
- This sculpture is important because Ft. Wayne wants to become a hub for creative expression with art, sculptures and wall murals located around the city

Artist Linda Howard:

Linda Howard resides in Bradenton, Florida and studied at the Art Institute of Chicago, Northwestern University and University of Denver.

She has been an artist for over forty-two years and has thirty-five sculptures and works of art located in 18 states and Australia.

Sculpture Design Concepts:

"It will be a nice area to be able to walk around, look up at and catch the light and shadow" —Linda Howard

The artist wanted visitors to be able to see the sculpture at night, so she used extensive lighting to illuminate the design.

"As one moves around the sculpture, one experiences a visual adventure, never seeing the same view twice. Light and shadows constantly change in the ambient light. The form relates to the rhythm of the water, the heartbeat of the three rivers, a crossroad and a powerful unifying force."

—Statement by Artist Linda Howard

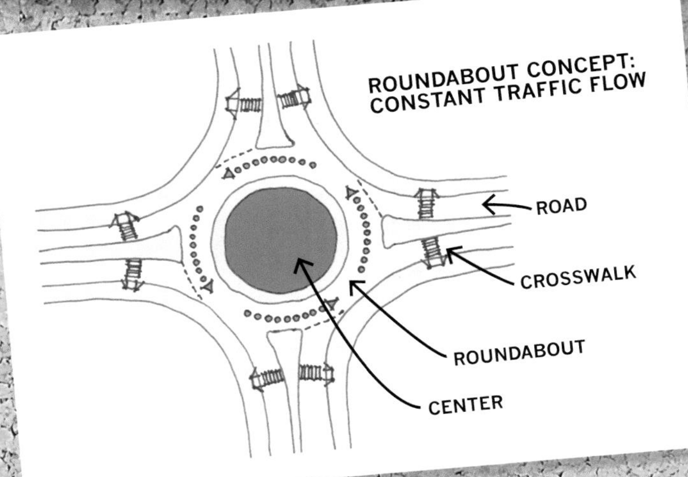

Public Art: "Roundabout Art"

Located in the center of traffic roundabouts in Carmel

1. **Location:** Horseferry Road (Villages of West Clay)—2001
Name of Art: Landscape with fountain—2016
Designer: Brunswick Development

2. **Location:** Main Street & Hazel Dell Parkway—1998
Name of Art: *Kick*—November 2017
Artist: Jorge Blanco—Sarasota, Florida

3. **Location:** 126th Street & Hazel Dell Parkway—1998
Name of Art: *Home Run*—November 2017
Artist: Jorge Blanco—Sarasota, Florida

4. **Location:** 96th St. & Westfield Blvd.—2005
Name of Art: *Beacon Bloom*—September 2017
Artist: Arlon Bayliss—Anderson, Indiana

I like to see art and sculptures when I'm out and about. It's fun to identify roundabout art when I'm riding around!

5. **Location:** Main Street & Keystone Parkway West—2010
Name of Art: *10 Galloping Greyhounds*—March 2018
Designer & Manufacturer: Bomar Industries

6. **Location:** 126th St. & Gray—2017
Name of Art: *Stone Paper Scissors*—August 2019
Artist: Kevin Box—Santa Fe, New Mexico

7. **Location:** Range Line Road & 4th St.—2017
Name of Art: *Reckon*—September 2019
Artist: Brad Howe, Los Angeles, California

8. **Location:** North Pennsylvania & Old Meridian St.—2007
Name of Art: *Grace, Love, & Joy*—September 2019
Artist: Arlon Bayliss—Anderson, Indiana

WHAT IS AN ARCHITECT & WHAT DO THEY DO?

LEARN THE PATH A KID—JUST LIKE YOU!—COULD TAKE TO BECOME AN ARCHITECT OR WORK IN THE DESIGN FIELD

What Is An Architect & What Do They Do?

- A problem solver who uses analytical & design process skills
- Plans & designs sites, campuses, houses & buildings
- Plans & designs exterior areas & urban areas
- Collaborates with designers and engineers to create projects
- Prepares documents that a general contractor uses to build
- Oversees the construction of projects

What Is The Path to Becoming An Architect?

- **Age 2-5:** Develop creative skills through play
- **Age 5-8:** Develop an interest in building toys/activities
- **Age 8-11:** Develop team building & collaboration skills
- **Age 11-14:** Begin to understand building design, functionality & styles
- **Age 14-18:** Understand the total design process
- Select & attend a school of architecture
- Internship in an architecture firm or related company
- Graduate from architecture school (in 5 to 6 years)
- Prepare for and pass the exam to become an architect

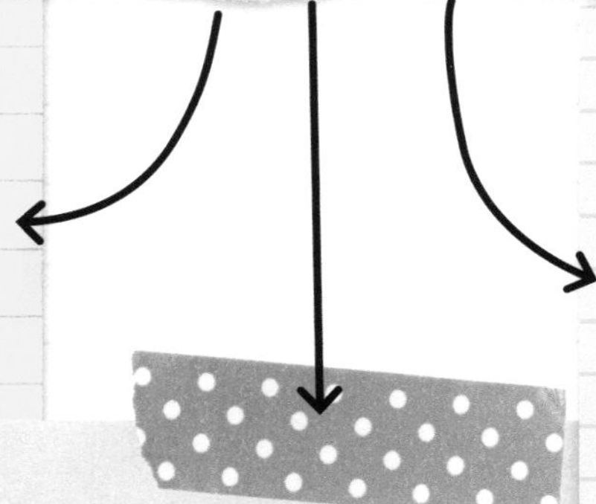

Roles & Jobs in Related Fields

- Work for an owner (typically in a design & construction department)
- Owner representative (during the duration of a project)
- Work for a general contractor or developer
- City/state building code agency official
- Product or service representative for the design industry
- Professor or teacher of architecture or design schools

Roles & Jobs in Architecture Firms

- Project Architect (working on all aspects of a project)
- Project Manager (manages internal & external team)
- Design Architect (working on the design of buildings)
- Technical Architect (working on how the buildings are built)
- Principal-in-Charge (manages client & team)
- Construction Observation & Administration
- Firm Leadership, Management or Finance

Roles & Jobs in Non-Traditional Fields

- Social & community advocate for architecture & development issues
- Governmental positions & political service
- Work in 3D or virtual presentation field
- Work for furniture or product manufacturer
- Work for architecture/design media publications

S.T.E.A.M. ACTIVITIES

SCIENCE, TECHNOLOGY, ENGINEERING, ARTS AND MATHEMATICS PROJECTS TO SUPPLEMENT THE TEXT

What Items Can I Use?

Find items that you already have around your house! It would be a great idea to keep the items in a central container for your child to use whenever they want to create! This can be their STEAM Container.

- ☐ tape
- ☐ painters tape
- ☐ toilet paper rolls
- ☐ paper towel rolls
- ☐ paper
- ☐ cardboard
- ☐ pipe cleaners
- ☐ blocks
- ☐ straws
- ☐ tooth picks
- ☐ water bottles
- ☐ string
- ☐ pencils
- ☐ plastic cups
- ☐ paper plates
- ☐ sponges
- ☐ rubber bands
- ☐ popsicle sticks
- ☐ scissors

Supporting Your Child's Challenges

- Begin the challenge by identifying the problem and what you want to achieve.
- Brainstorm how you can achieve the solution.
- No ideas are too silly or impossible. Encourage your child to get creative!
- Remember failure is a part of the process. Encourage your child to work through their challenges and find a creative solution!

Questions to Ask After the STEAM Project

- What are the architectural features of the project?
- What are the building features of the project?
- What would you do differently?
- What did you learn from your failures? From your success?

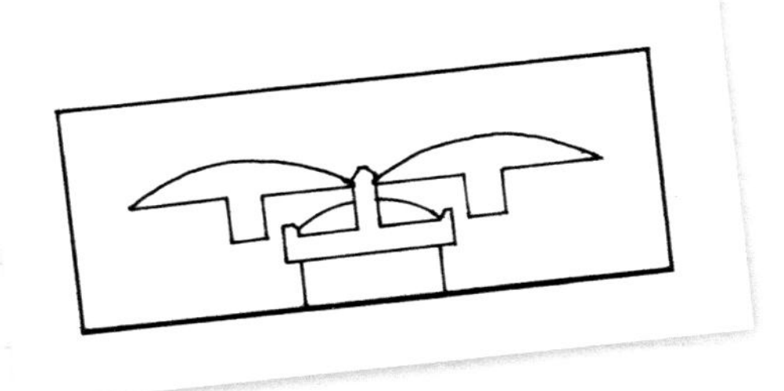

FIRST NAME: ____________ AGE: ______ DATE: ________ STATE: ____________

LUCAS OIL STADIUM

Completed in 2008

Lucas Oil Stadium is home to the Indianapolis Colts football team. Every home game is played at the stadium. One of its most well-known features is its retractable roof.

- **Goal**: Your task is to create a building with a retractable roof.
- **Think About Your Structure**: You will need to create a sturdy base before adding on the retractable roof.
- **Hint**: How will you get the roof to move? Will you use a pulley system or some kind of roller to move the roof? There are lots of ways to move the roof, so be creative!
- **Now What?** Think about how long it takes to move the roof. Is it an easy function or does it take a lot of time? Why would a retractable roof be beneficial for a building and its occupants?

____

____

____

- Legos
- cardboard
- tape
- string

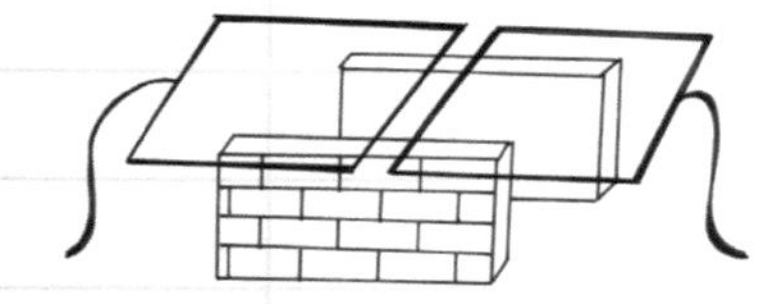

Kid Architect's sketch

Draw your sketch here

If you would like to share your work, upload it to my Facebook page: KidArchitectBook

©Kid Architect Book

FIRST NAME: ______________________ AGE: ______ DATE: __________ STATE: ______________

PUBLIC ART: "LOVE" SCULPTURE

Completed in 1970

The "LOVE" sculpture is public art that spells out the letters in the word love, L-O-V-E.

- **Goal**: Think of an important word in your life. Some examples could be family, friends, happiness. Use one word and create your own sculpture using those letters.
- **Think About Your Sculpture**: Will you use a formal lettering to design your sculpture or will it be handwritten?
- **Hint**: Make this sculpture meaningful to you!
- **Now What?** Where would you put this sculpture on display? Would you put it near a school or park or would you keep it closer to yourself and put it in your yard?

____

____

____

- paper towel roll
- ribbon
- blocks
- tooth picks

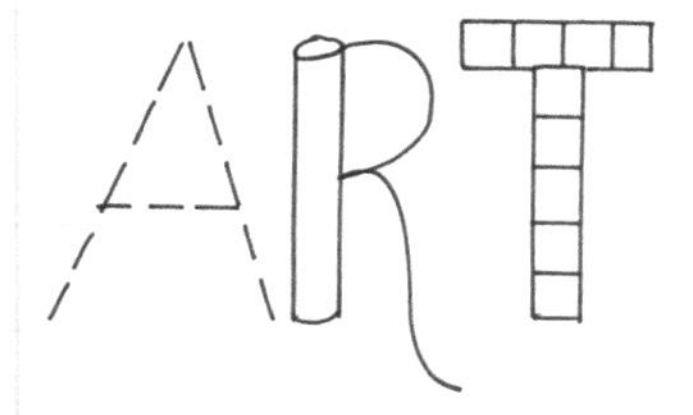

Kid Architect's sketch

Draw your sketch here

If you would like to share your work, upload it to my Facebook page: KidArchitectBook

©Kid Architect Book

GLOSSARY OF LANDSCAPE, ARCHITECTURE, AND BUILDING TERMS

ACTIVE LEARNING CLASSROOM
A large multifunctional and flexible space where teaching strives to involve students in the learning process more directly than other methods. The method includes activities where the students are doing rather than passively listening.

ARCHITECT
A person who conceives, plans and designs houses, buildings and structures. In addition, they oversee the construction when the design is being built. An architect is required to have a professional license to practice architecture in the United States.

ARTIFACTS
Elements of houses and buildings that are a part of the building but do not provide any structural or required portion of the building. Examples of artifacts include those exterior and interior items which can be removed and assist in explaining the story and history of the house or building. Typically, artifacts are included in historic and older houses and buildings.

ATRIUM
A large open area within a house or building which is generally taller than one story and includes mechanical, electrical, plumbing and ventilation systems.

AUDITORIUM
A large building or interior space of a building which is multifunctional. It may be used as a theater, concert hall, public gathering place, and for stage performances and speeches. It is typically a space which can seat many people.

BEAM
A long and heavy timber, stone or steel element used as a major support for a building. Generally, a beam spans between two columns and is integral to form a structural system of a building.

Here's a selection of words that might be new to you. If you see a word you don't know the meaning of, this is a good place to start. -Kid Architect

CIVIL ENGINEER
The specialty of engineering involved with design and engineering that coordinates the below grade and above grade elements of a site/earth including infrastructure, roads, parking, bridges, buildings and structures.

COLUMN
A vertical or pillar type member that supports beams and is used as a major support for a building. Generally, a column is one floor in height and is integral to form a structural system of a building.

CONFLUENCE
The junction or joining of two or more rivers to form one larger river.

CONSULTING ENGINEER
An engineer who provides professional advice, expertise or services for the design and construction industry.

COR-TEN STEEL
A weathering and low carbon product. This steel has a small amount of copper and other elements added which causes the steel to have an outer layer patina that provides a rusted look.

COURTYARD
An enclosed yard or space with no roof. This can be either within or adjacent to a building.

DOME
A circular vault usually in the form of a sphere which is open with no visible structure supporting it. The exterior of a dome is usually designed to reflect that it is a special element of the building. In addition, the interior design of the ceiling of a dome is usually ornate and expressive.

ELECTRICAL ENGINEER
A person involved in the specialty of engineering that involves the design and coordination of the electrical and power systems of a house, building or structure.

ENGINEER
A person who plans and designs below ground systems, structures, building systems and other related building elements. When engineers are involved in the design and construction of houses, buildings and structures; they normally practice a specific type of engineering.

GENERAL CONTRACTOR

A company who agrees, by contract, to do specific work or supply goods for a certain price. A general contractor is the company which constructs houses, buildings and structures designed by an architect.

GOLDEN DOME

The name for the main administration building on the campus of Notre Dame University. The name comes from the color of the dome, which includes flecks of real gold.

INFRASTRUCTURE

The basic facilities and systems of building support which are necessary to operate a house, building or structure. This includes systems which are both below ground and above ground. The systems defined as infrastructure include electrical, sewer, storm, water and natural gas.

MARQUEE

Most commonly a structure or sign located over the entrance to a theater. It either identifies the name of the theater or identifies the event or events currently booked at that theater.

MECHANICAL ENGINEER

The specialty of engineering involved with the design of the heating, ventilating and air conditioning systems (HVAC) for buildings and structures.

REFURBISHMENT

A smaller or reduced process of renovation. A refurbishment typically does not move any walls or doors and involves only the change of interior finishes of a house or building.

RENDERING

An image of either an exterior or interior of a building showing the attributes of an architectural design. A rendering can be either illustrated as a freehand drawing or computer generated.

RESEARCH

The systematic investigation and study to obtain and analyze information such as theory, event, intellectual discipline or similar items. Research is then applied to the planning, design and construction of houses, buildings and structures.

RESORT HOTEL

A building located in a special place to go to for rest, relaxation and respite. Generally, a resort hotel includes additional amenities and activities for guests to enjoy and engage.

KNUTE ROCKNE (1888-1931)

A Norwegian-American football player and coach at the University of Notre Dame. He is known as being one of the greatest coaches in college football history for popularizing the forward pass. He died in 1931 in a tragic airplane crash.

STAGE

A multifunctional space used for the performance of theatrical productions, musical performances, presentations and teaching. It is a large open space to allow for many different uses.

STEEL

An alloy of iron and carbon along with other elements. Its high tensile strength and low cost is why it is used in buildings, infrastructure, tools, ships, automobiles, machines and appliances.

STRUCTURAL REINFORCED CONCRETE

Structural concrete that contains steel bars to increase its strength and prevent cracks in the concrete, thus, increasing its useful life.

TRUSSES

A structural beam utilized to support long spans to create large open spaces below. The most common use of trusses is in buildings to support roofs and floors because they are lightweight and can support heavy loads.

ZONING CODE

To divide an area of a city, town, neighborhood or assembly of projects in order to control its design and development by rules, regulations and guidelines.

The authors from L to R:
Elizabeth Wells, Lauren Vance & Gary Vance

GARY VANCE, FAIA is an architect who has been in professional practice for over 40 years. He is nationally known for his expertise in the planning and design of healthcare and wellness campuses and facilities. He has been elected to the College of Fellows of the American Institute of Architects. In addition, he has been elected to the College of Fellows of the American College of Healthcare Architects. A graduate of the College of Architecture and Planning at Ball State University, Gary is a recipient of the Distinguished Alumni Award.

LAUREN VANCE is a freelance graphic designer with over fourteen years of experience in marketing and design based in Cleveland, Ohio. She lives there with her husband, two young children, and ornery kitten. She is a graduate of Miami University in Oxford, Ohio with a B.F.A in Graphic Design.

ELIZABETH WELLS is a former elementary school teacher of ten years. She lives in Westfield, Indiana with her husband, son, daughter and dog. She graduated from Ball State University with both a B.S. and M.S. in Elementary Education.

PHOTOGRAPHY CREDITS BY PAGE

Photos are listed clockwise from the top left of the spread. All stock imagery rights owned by the author.

Front Cover:

Purdue University Smoke Stack Rendering: Courtesy of BSA Lifestructures
Mother Mary Statue: By iStock
Emens Auditorium: Courtesy of Denise Vance
Indianapolis Children's Museum: Courtesy of Susan Fleck
Wilmeth Active Learning Center: Courtesy of BSA Lifestructures
Lucas Oil Stadium: Courtesy of Denise Vance

Pages 4–5:

Exterior photo by iStock
Historical postcard is a public domain image
Exterior photo by iStock
Statue photo by iStock
Small interior photo courtesy of Susan Fleck
Small exterior photo courtesy of Susan Fleck

Pages 6–7:

Exterior photo is a public domain image
Albright photo is a public domain image
Interior photo by Susan Fleck
Historical postcard is a public domain image
Interior photo by Susan Fleck
Houston Astrodome photo is a public domain image

Pages 8–9:

All Boone County Courthouse photos courtesy of Denise Vance
West Baden Spring Hotel interior photo by Susan Fleck

Pages 10–11:

Exterior photo courtesy of Immortal Images, Howard Doughty—Bay Village, Ohio
Marquee image courtesy of Denise Vance
Rendering courtesy of Cripe Design & Leedy/Cripe Architects
Interior photo courtesy of Immortal Images, Howard Doughty—Bay Village, Ohio

Pages 12–13:

Exterior photo courtesy of Alex Vertikoff
Interior photo courtesy of Alex Vertikoff
Frank Lloyd Wright photo by Alamy
Interior photo courtesy of Alex Vertikoff

Pages 14–15:

Color exterior photo courtesy of Gary Vance
Color interior photo is a public domain image
Black and white exterior photo by Ball State University archives
Black and white interior photo by Ball State University archives
Color interior photo by Ball State University archives
Black and white interior photo by Ball State University archives
Ball jar photo courtesy of Denise Vance

Pages 16–17:

Exterior daytime photos courtesy of Don Nissen, Columbus Area Visitors Center
Exterior night photo by Esto Photographs
Black and white interior photo courtesy of Korab, CIAA (Columbus Indiana Architectural Archives)

Pages 18–19:

All Assembly Hall building photos courtesy of Susan Fleck

Pages 20–21:

Exterior photo courtesy of Michael Firsich
Louis Kahn photo by Alamy
Interior photo courtesy of Daniel Overbey
Building rendering courtesy of Daniel Overbey
Interior photo courtesy of Daniel Overbey

Pages 22–23:

All Children's Museum of Indianapolis building interior and exterior photos courtesy of Susan Fleck
Carousel photo courtesy of Children's Museum of Indianapolis

Pages 24–25:

All Falls of the Ohio Interpretive Center photos courtesy of Woolpert
Aerial photo courtesy of Google Maps

Pages 26–27:

All White Chapel interior and exterior photos courtesy of Bryan Cantwell

Pages 28–29:

Exterior photo courtesy of Denise Vance
Manning statue photo courtesy of Denise Vance
All additional photos are public domain images
Aerial map courtesy of Google Maps

Pages 30–31:

All Evansville Museum of Arts, History & Science photos courtesy of Susan Fleck.

Page 32-33:

All Wilmeth Active Learning Center building photos and smoke stack rendering courtesy of BSA Lifestructures

Page 34:

Sculpture photos courtesy of Susan Fleck
LOVE stamp image by iStock

Page 35:

Winter photo courtesy of Denise Vance
Summer photo by iStock

Page 36:

Nighttime photo is a public domain image
Daytime Convergence sculpture photos courtesy of Michael Firsich

Page 37:

All Carmel Roundabout Art photos courtesy of Michael Firsich

Page 44:

Author photo courtesy of Denise Vance

Back Cover:

Indianapolis Children's Museum photo courtesy of Susan Fleck